THE MONSTER FROM UNDERGROUND

This edition first published in Great Britain 2000 by Mammoth
First published in Great Britain 1990 by Heinemann Young Books
imprints of Egmont Children's books Ltd, a division of Egmont Holding Ltd
239 Kensington High St, London W8 6SA
Published in hardback by Heinemann Library, a division of Reed Educational and
Professional Publishing Ltd, by arrangement with Egmont Children's Books Ltd.
Text copyright © Gillian Cross 1990
Illustrations copyright © Chris Priestley 2000
The author and illustrator have asserted their moral rights.
Paperback ISBN 0 7497 4227 5
Hardback ISBN 0 431 06185 8
10 9 8 7 6 5 4 3 2 1
A CIP catalogue record for this title is available from the British Library.
Printed in Dubai.

THE MONSTER FROM UNDERGROUND

GILLIAN CROSS
Illustrated by Chris Priestley

🍌 YELLOW BANANAS

To Anthony

G.C.

For Glenn

C.P.

Chapter One

BOMBER WILSON WAS brilliant. He was a wonderful footballer, a star at snooker and a genius at video games. He knew about computers and aeroplanes and dinosaurs and he had the best bicycle in the whole school.

But he HATED writing.

Whenever Mrs Evans, his teacher, said, 'Get out your pens,' Bomber shuddered. He could never write more than a quarter of a page, about anything. After that, his hand ached from holding the pen, and his brain ached even more.

So he was horrified when Mrs Evans told them about the Nature Diary.

'First,' she said, 'choose something to watch for a week. Write a little bit about it every day – just before you go to bed.'

For a week! Bomber shuddered.

'Can we watch anything we like?' said Kevin.

Harriet Newton tossed her head. '*I'm* going to make a rain gauge to put in my garden. Then I can write about the weather every day. How much rain there's been and –'

'I'll watch my dog,' Paul said, interrupting. They all interrupted Harriet, because she never stopped. 'I'll notice what he does every day.'

Mrs Evans beamed. 'That's the idea. Watch for seven days – and keep an open mind. Then at the end of the week, write down what you've learnt. There'll be a prize for the best one.'

Seven days' writing! At home! Bomber sat and glowered as everyone chattered about the Diaries. And by the end of the day, he was the only person in the class who hadn't had an idea.

'Look for something interesting on your way home,' Mrs Evans said.

So he looked hard. And what he saw was the road works.

They were making a cutting through Hawthorn Hill, for the new motorway, and all the different

levels of rock showed. Just like layers in a slice of cake, except that each layer of rock was older than the one above.

Bomber stared at them. Those rocks had been hidden under the ground for millions and millions of years and suddenly there they were, up on top again. Now that *was* interesting.

And perhaps he could write about it in his Nature Diary! He grinned and got the book out, to make a sketch.

But Harriet was right behind him, and she hooted with laughter. 'Hey, everyone! Bomber's going to write a Nature Diary about a *road works*!'

'It's the rocks not the road works,' said Bomber.

But Harriet didn't listen. She just laughed louder. 'Watch those diggers, Bomber! Perhaps one of them will have a dear little baby digger! Or spin a web and catch an aeroplane!'

'Shut up!' said Bomber.

But Harriet went on about vegetarian tractors and wild, meat-eating diggers, all the way home. And it *was* all the way, because she lived next door to Bomber.

So he didn't have a moment to think about his Nature Diary.

Chapter Two

THE NEXT DAY was Tuesday, and Mrs Evans kept nagging him about choosing something for the Diary. But he couldn't think of a thing.

To make it worse, Harriet spent all day teasing him about diggers. She even kept it up while they walked home, which made him rush past the road works without stopping.

And that was a pity, because the machines had opened up a whole new layer since the day before. Quite a different sort of rock, with some strange, interesting-looking lumps in it. But Bomber didn't look properly, because of Harriet.

When he got home –
there was Harriet's mother,
drinking coffee and going
on about the rain gauge.

Bomber's mother
frowned as he came in.
'What are *you* doing for
this Nature Diary, Bernard?'

'I'm still deciding.'
Bomber shuffled his feet.

Mrs Newton rattled on
without taking any notice,
just like Harriet.

' . . . and she checks that gauge every five
minutes, to see how much rain she's collected.
I had to *make* her go to bed last night.'

That was when Bomber had his idea. If Mrs
Newton *made* Harriet go to bed at night – he
would do his Nature Diary then! He could slip
out every night, at midnight, and do a survey of
the night sky! If he did it at night, he wouldn't
have to put up with Harriet laughing at him
over the fence.

Brilliant! He didn't tell his mother, of course, but he set the alarm on his watch straight away.

It woke him up at a quarter to midnight, beeping quietly in his ear. By five to twelve he was standing in the back garden, looking up at the sky.

Half the sky. The other half was hidden by the Newtons' apple tree. He needed to climb higher to get a proper view. Standing on the rubbish heap, he scrambled on to the shed roof and took a good look around.

That was when he saw them.

There were three roundish grey things, lying in a patch of moonlight in the middle of Harriet's lawn. They were as big as footballs, but not quite ball-shaped. More like eggs.

Eggs? How could they be? What creature laid eggs the size of footballs?

All the lights were off in the Newtons' house. Quietly, Bomber slid down into their garden and walked across the lawn, to have a better look at the strange grey objects.

They were definitely eggs. Huge, *enormous* eggs. He put out his hand to feel the shells, but just before he touched them he noticed something else. Something that made him snatch his hand back, as fast as he could.

Footprints.

There were two of them. They were at least half a metre long, and deep as well, as if they'd been made by something very heavy.

Between them was a long, deep groove, like the mark of a dragging tail.

Except that this tail had to be the size of a tree trunk.

Bomber stared. It was frightening, standing next to those giant eggs and looking at those enormous footprints – but it was a brilliant chance to begin his Nature Diary. He began to sketch the eggs and the footprints, as fast as he could.

Then a voice hissed behind him. 'What are you doing?'

He turned round and saw Harriet, glaring at him.

'Have you been fiddling with my rain gauge?' she snapped.

'Your rain gauge?' Bomber almost laughed. 'Who cares about that? Just look at these amazing eggs. And the footprints.'

'Eggs?' Harriet said.  'Footprints? What are you talking about?'

'You must be blind! Can't you see –' Bomber whirled around, to point at them – and stopped dead.

There was only the empty lawn. The eggs and the footprints had vanished.

Chapter Three

THE NEXT DAY, Harriet's father came round as soon as he got home from work. To complain.

'Bernard's been tampering with Harriet's rain gauge.'

It was no use arguing. Bomber's mother wouldn't listen. She lost her temper and sent him straight to bed.

Bomber pulled a face, but he was really quite tired. He lay down on the bed to read a comic and fell asleep at once, without undressing or pulling the curtains.

When his alarm went off at a quarter to
twelve, he woke up and blinked. For a moment
he couldn't think what was going on, because
he had forgotten all about the survey of the
night sky. And then, suddenly, he was wide
awake.

Something had moved, just outside the
window.

There was no shape to be seen. Just darkness.
But the darkness had rippled and *moved*.

For a few seconds, Bomber was too frightened
to breathe. Then the rippling happened again.

19

Very slowly, as if something was crawling past the window. On and on and on.

But it was an *upstairs* window! What was huge enough to block that? It would have to be bigger than an elephant!

Whatever it was, it wasn't looking in. Quietly he crawled out of bed and crept over to the window. Pressing his nose to the glass, he peered out at the stuff that was passing. It was rough and wrinkled, a bit like an elephant's

skin. And where the moonlight caught it, he could see blotches and streaks.

Bomber's heart thudded with fright, but he wouldn't let himself run back to bed. Whatever the creature was, it was much too big to get into the room. It was worth trying to get a better look at it.

Carefully, Bomber pulled down the window catch. It squeaked a bit, but whatever was outside didn't take any notice. The skin just went on rippling past as he pushed the window open.

The smell nearly
knocked him over.

It was like old grass
cuttings and rotting
plants, mixed with
mushrooms and stale
cabbage.

Bomber clapped
his hand over his nose
but, before he could recover, the door behind
him was flung open. His mother appeared in

her dressing gown,
looking angry.

'Bernard, what
are you doing? You
woke me up from
a deep sleep!'

Hadn't she
noticed the smell?
Bomber waved at
the window. 'Look!'

'At what?' said
his mother.

Bomber turned back to the window, but there was no smell any more. No rough, blotchy skin. Just the dark sky, with the moon shining through the Newtons' apple tree.

The giant whatever-it-was had vanished.

His mother made him go to bed at once, but the moment she was out of the way, he switched on his bedside light. Very strange things were happening, and he wanted to make sure he remembered them. Grabbing his Nature Diary, he started to write.

I have just seen something very peculiar outside my window . . .

Chapter Four

ON THURSDAY, BOMBER made a plan. He knew it was no use trying to tell people about the eggs and the wrinkled skin and the giant footprints. No one would believe a word of it.

He needed a witness.

Next time something strange happened, there had to be someone else there. Not one of his friends. Someone who wouldn't back him up unless he was telling the truth.

And he knew the ideal person.

At twenty to twelve that night, he was standing in the Newtons' back garden, throwing little stones up at Harriet's window to wake her up.

It worked brilliantly, because the window was open. Harriet stuck her head out, looking furious.

'*Bomber?* What's going on? That hit me on the nose.'

'Sssh!' Bomber said. 'Come down.'

'Why? If you've touched my rain gauge –'

Bomber didn't bother to answer. He just backed away from the window and waited, staring up at the big, bright moon behind the apple tree. After a few minutes, Harriet crept through the back door.

'Are you crazy?' she hissed. 'My dad'll go berserk if he catches you in our garden again. What do you want?'

'Wait a bit, and I'll show you,' muttered Bomber. 'And be quiet.'

They waited. They stood with their backs to the house, staring down the hill. Far below, they could see the motorway road works but even those were still and quiet.

25

'It's funny,' Harriet whispered. 'Everything's very bright, but there's no moon.'

'Yes there is,' said Bomber. 'Up behind the apple tree. It —'

And then he stopped. Because she was right. There wasn't a moon behind the apple tree, and there weren't any stars either. Instead, there was a big, black patch, as if something was standing between them and the sky. Something huge.

'Harriet —'

But before he could warn her, the black shape moved and they saw it properly. The monster. It had a vast, humped body and a long, thick neck that reared up into the sky. Its head looked ridiculously small as it peered over the top of the house.

Harriet gasped. She clutched at Bomber's arm and he clutched hers.

Slowly, the small head swayed from side to side, and they caught a whiff of the mushroomy, rotten-grass smell.

Then Harriet gulped. 'Look at the apple tree!'

The creature's head bent down to grab at the top of the tree and the leaves shook, furiously.

When the head reared up again, there were black, leafy shapes sticking out of its mouth. A slow crunching, chomping sound came from somewhere up in the sky.

Bomber didn't dare to move, but he stared at the little head and the long, long neck. They reminded him of something. If only he could work out what . . .

And then − it vanished.

Suddenly, there was nothing there, except the big, white moon, behind the black branches of the apple tree. Harriet took a deep breath.

'What *was* it?'

'I don't know,' said Bomber. 'But I'm certainly going to find out.'

When he got back to his bedroom, he wrote down all the details, underneath what he had written the day before.

. . . its body must have been six or seven metres high, and its neck reached even higher. It was a very long, thin neck, with a small head . . .

He lay awake for hours, trying to think where he had seen a neck and a head like that. But his brain refused to work. He fell asleep at half past four, without having remembered.

But when he woke up the next morning, he *knew*.

He jumped out of bed and rummaged in the bottom of his wardrobe. There was a great

heap of polythene bags in there, full of old toys
and games. Building bricks. Plastic aeroplanes.
Model soldiers with their trucks and weapons.
And somewhere . . .

The bag he was looking for was right at the
bottom. He tugged it out and emptied it on to
the floor.

There were dozens of little plastic dinosaurs,
all different shapes and colours. He shuffled
through them, tossing away the stegosaurus and
the tyrannosaurus, the parasaurolophus and the
iguanadon.

And suddenly, there was the one he was looking for. He gazed at the long neck and the little head for a moment, and then turned it over to read the name underneath, to make sure he was right.

DIPLODOCUS.

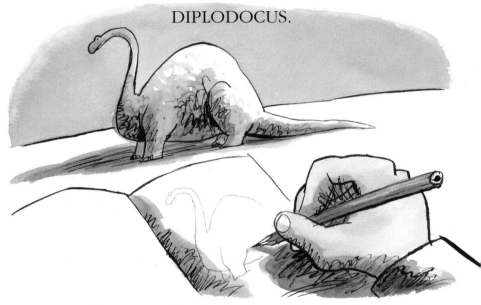

Standing it on his bedside table, he sketched the shape carefully in his Nature Diary. Then he pushed it into his pocket. All the way to school, his fingers were curled round the thick body, feeling the long, long neck and the long, long tail.

Was it *possible*?

As he passed the road works, he stopped for a minute or two, to look at the layers of rock in the cutting. The bottom layer was a long way down. It must be very old. And he could still see those strange lumps in it . . .

When he got to school, he didn't say anything to Harriet. He just took out the diplodocus and pushed it into her hand.

She stared. 'But that's impossible. They've been extinct for millions of years.'

'I know,' Bomber said. 'But look at it.'

Harriet looked down at the dinosaur again. 'Nobody will believe us,' she said. 'Unless we can prove it. How about a photograph?'

Bomber stared. Then, for the first time ever, he smiled at her. 'Brilliant! Let's do it tonight.'

Chapter Five

THEY MET IN Harriet's back garden just before midnight, both carrying their cameras.

'We'll get better pictures if we're high up,' muttered Harriet. 'Because the creature's so big. Let's climb onto your shed.'

They knelt on the roof, side by side, with the cameras held ready. At first they thought nothing was going to happen, but after ten minutes, Bomber nudged Harriet.

The apple tree was shaking. The fluttering leaves showed up clearly, with the full moon behind them. And then, slowly – very slowly – the huge black shape of the diplodocus began to move.

Bomber shivered. Suppose the monster saw them? Suppose it knocked the shed over? Suppose –

But it was no good thinking about that. If they wanted photographs, they had to stay there. He forced himself to hold the camera steady.

'Now!' hissed Harriet.

Both cameras flashed at once. The light was like an explosion, much brighter than Bomber had expected. It must have surprised the diplodocus too. Slowly, but not quite as slowly as before, it moved again – towards them.

Its head reared up, on top of its long neck, and began to sway from side to side, searching. Getting closer and closer. Harriet gulped.

'Let's get out of here!'

Bomber shook his head. 'Wait. I don't think it'll hurt us. It's supposed to be a vegetarian.' Crossing his fingers hard, he hoped all those scientists were right.

The head swayed closer and closer. It was small for such a huge animal – but it looked enormous as it came down towards them. Lower and lower it bent, until Bomber and Harriet were looking straight into its eyes.

The eyes of a dinosaur.

They were very pale, like pools of rainwater, and empty. Bomber stared deep into them. He couldn't tell whether the diplodocus saw them, but he was too scared to move.

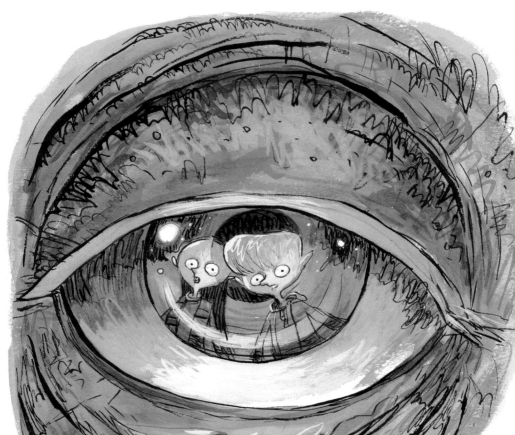

Then Harriet grabbed his arm. 'Photos!' she whispered. 'We'll never get another chance like this.'

Both together, they lifted their cameras. Bomber got the focus right and made sure the dinosaur's head was in the centre of his viewfinder. Then he said, 'Now!'

And the flashes went off together.

What happened then was mind-boggling.

Bomber wrote it all down in his Nature Diary the next morning.

. . . when the lights flashed, the dinosaur began to move towards us again. We couldn't escape, because it was too close. For one second, we could see it lurching forwards and then everything went dark and very strange. Tingling.

The diplodocus walked straight through us.

Chapter Six

HARRIET GOT THE photos developed on Saturday morning, and she took them straight round to Bomber's. When he opened the door, he could see that she was upset.

'What's the matter, Harry?'

'It's these. Look.' She held out the photographs.

There were four beautiful pictures of the full moon behind the apple tree – but no sign of a dinosaur in any of them.

'There's nothing there,' said Harriet. 'Did we imagine it?'

Bomber shook his head. 'I don't think so. Come down to the road works. I want to show you something.'

They walked down together to the cutting in Hawthorn Hill and stared at the layers of rock. Like layers in a slice of cake – except that each one was older than the one above.

'The bottom layer must be very old indeed,' Harriet said slowly.

Bomber nodded. 'About a hundred and fifty million years.'

'And those strange, enormous lumps?'

'Bones,' said Bomber. 'I reckon.'

Harriet frowned. 'Someone ought to have a look at them.'

'I've been thinking about that,' said Bomber. 'I think I'll write to the local paper.'

'Write? *You?*'

Harriet hooted with laughter, but Bomber just grinned.

Chapter Seven

TWO WEEKS LATER, Bomber finished his
Nature Diary. First he pasted in the best of his
newspaper cuttings. There was a large
photograph of his face and underneath it said:

Bernard 'Bomber' Wilson

Diplodocus

SCHOOLBOY'S DINOSAUR FIND

Schoolboy Bernard Wilson (above left) has
sharp eyes! He noticed some strange lumps
in the excavation for the new M39 and wrote
to his local paper about them. Now scientists
believe that the lumps are fossilized bones of a
diplodocus (above right) — a huge dinosaur that
has been extinct for millions of years.

There was a sketch of the diplodocus, too. The artist had got the face a bit wrong and drawn the skin all scaly, but it was definitely the creature they had seen in Harriet's garden.

When he had stuck the cutting in, Bomber read through the whole Diary again. He was amazed to see how much he had written. There was only one page left, and he knew what had to go on that. Picking up his pen, he began to write.

WHAT I'VE LEARNT

I'm sure we saw a diplodocus. Not a real one, because someone else would have noticed that. And a live diplodocus couldn't have walked through us.

I think it was a ghost. It started walking when its bones came to the surface in the road works. And it's stopped now the bones have been discovered.

I've thought a lot about this, Mrs Evans. Keeping an open mind, like you said. And I can't see any other explanation.

Mrs Evans was delighted with Bomber's Diary.

Well done! she wrote underneath. *It's crazy but it's brilliant. And at last you've managed to write a lot!*

And she gave him two gold stars and a special prize for the Most Original Entry.

She didn't say she believed Bomber's story, but she kept the newspaper cutting. And she promised the class a trip to see the dinosaur.

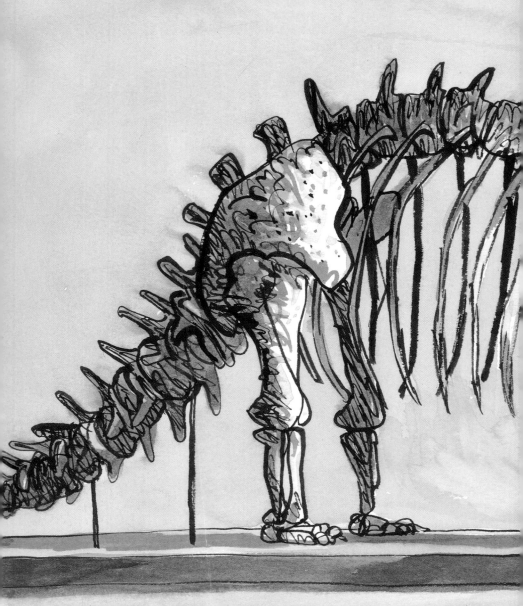

Diplodocus

YELLOW BANANAS

Yellow Bananas are brilliantly imaginative stories written by some of today's top writers. These beautifully illustrated books provide an excellent introduction to chapter books.

So if you've enjoyed this story, why not pick another from the bunch?

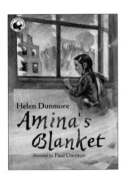

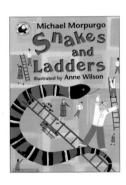